D1548442

About the Book

Russell Hoban has created a joyous fantasy for young children, a spring-time celebration complete with pastoral songs, sprightly characters, and pungent Hoban humor.

Letitia Rabbit is to play the legendary Miss Green, harbinger of spring, in the annual Birch Hollow String Festival. But like everyone else in Birch Hollow, Letitia is worried, for it doesn't seem as if winter is *ever* going to end.

When Letitia meets the *real* Miss Green, she finds that she is worried too, for blustery Mr. Brumus (the spirit of winter, who holds her in his power through the icy months of the year) is not about to give up his control of the winter weather vane. And Miss Green is too tired to find the song that will relax his grip and put him to sleep!

Spring can't arrive on time without the right song, and Miss Green hopes that Letitia Rabbit will be able to help her find the necessary song before it is too late.

Mary Chalmers' soft, luminous, watercolor drawings perfectly picture Letitia's quest, delicately creating a springtime world of the imagination that children will treasure.

COWARD, McCANN & GEOGHEGAN, INC.
NEW YORK

Letitia Rabbit's String Song

by Russell Hoban

Illustrated by Mary Chalmers

JE

To Spring
and all my children

Was winter going to go away or wasn't it? Everybody in Birch Hollow was beginning to wonder. The annual String Festival was only a few weeks away, but the wind was cold, the sky was gray, and there was still snow on the ground.

"Winter's *got* to go," said Mrs. Rabbit with her mouth full of pins. "It always does. Hold still, Letitia, or I'll never get the hem right."

"I *am* holding still," said Letitia as she stopped turning around in front of the mirror. She was going to be Miss Green, the String Lady in the Birch Hollow String Festival, and she was going to wear the same pretty green dress her mother had worn when she had been Miss Green.

"Was there ever a real Miss Green?" asked Letitia. "I mean, was there ever a String Lady who really made the trees and the flowers and winter-sleeping animals wake up? Not just somebody one day a year in the Festival?"

"I don't honestly know," said Mrs. Rabbit. "Mr. First Selectrabbit Largehop might be able to tell you. I believe it was his great-great-great-grandfather who first brought the string to Birch Hollow."

"I'm going to ask him if I can borrow the string to practice with," said Letitia, "and I'll ask him that too." She took off the dress so her mother could finish it and hopped down to the Town Hall, which was in a thicket by an oak tree.

"You may borrow the string," said Mr. Largehop, "but you must be careful not to lose it. This very same ball of string has been used in the Festival ever since my great-great-great-grandfather's time."

"Is it a magic string?" asked Letitia. "Did he get it from the real Miss Green who wakes up trees and flowers and brings warm

breezes?" In the String Festival Miss Green always threw the ball of string while holding onto one end of it. Then the Birch Hollow rabbit hopped off with the ball, unwinding it and bringing string to Birch Hollow. Mr. Largehop's son Howard was going to be the Birch Hollow rabbit this year.

"Well," said Mr. Largehop, "it's a very special string, but I wouldn't say there's any magic about it. My great-great-great-grandfather came home one day with a ball of string, and it seems he said something about a lady in a green dress, and then the weather changed. Rabbits were a lot simpler in those days, and they had a big celebration. Ever since then we've had the String Festival. Everyone enjoys it and I get a chance to make a speech, which always pleases me. And of course Miss Green *is* real in a way, you might say — she's the spirit of string in Birch Hollow, and that's what you'll be in this year's Festival. If winter ever goes away so string can come." He gave Letitia the wooden box that had the ball of string inside it.

"Thank you, Mr. Largehop," said Letitia. She went home with the string, singing:

*String, string, the birds will sing
A new song when I hop along
The flowers to bring,
The blue skies and the breezes of
The happy days of string.*

The gray sky didn't look much like happy days, but Letitia was going to be Miss Green, and she was sure that the weather would change in time for string.

When Letitia got home she went to a little hill behind the house where she could be alone, and there she took the ball of string from the box. It was a thick, strong, green string that did not look old at all.

Letitia held the end of the string tightly. Then she said, in a high sweet voice that she thought was dignified and right for Miss Green, "String, string, go and bring leaves and flowers and balmy breezes." Then she threw the ball of string.

When the ball of string hit the ground it bounded away, rolling and bouncing down the hill and across a field. Letitia waited for it to stop, but it kept going. She stood there holding the end of the string,

feeling it shake and pull. Now the ball of string was out of sight and still rolling. Letitia tied her end around a tree and ran into the house.

"The ball of string rolled away," she said to her mother. "It rolled right down the hill and across a field and away."

"Well, go get it," said Mrs. Rabbit, and went on ironing the green dress.

Letitia went outside again. She felt a little nervous as she untied the quivering string from the tree. Holding it tightly, she began to wind it up as she followed it down the hill, across the field, and away. By now the other end might be somewhere she had never been, she thought, and the ball of string was still rolling on and growing smaller and smaller.

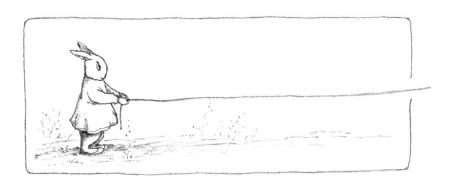

"A *plain* ball of string would have stopped long ago or got caught in brambles or something," said Letitia. "I wish I'd never borrowed that string." She stopped and tried to wind it in while standing still, but the string would not come. It stretched taut, as if it were snagged on something and would break if she pulled too hard. When she walked after it again, it was quite easy to wind it in.

Letitia walked through woods and over fields, crossing streams and climbing hills as she wound in the string. She kept walking and winding, but even after what seemed a very long time the ball of wound-up string was still very small, not even half as big as it had been to start with. "I believe that string is *stretching*, too," said Letitia. "I wonder if I'll get home before dark?"

By the time the ball of string looked almost as big as it had been
to start with night was coming on, and Letitia was very nervous and

unhappy. She followed the string through dark trees, looking all around her, sniffing the air and listening after every step. The air smelled like snow. She went up a hill, and at the top of it she saw a tall white house glimmering in the dusk behind tall green fir trees and a high yew hedge. There were lights in all the windows that she could see.

The string went under a black iron gate in the hedge. Letitia opened the gate and went down a walk between yew trees clipped into the shapes of giant wolves and bears and owls, all glittering with frost. She followed the string to a white door with a black iron knocker in the shape of a face with puffed-out cheeks blowing a black iron wind from its mouth. The end of the string was wrapped around the knocker, and as Letitia pulled to wind it in the knocker lifted and dropped with a bang.

The door was opened by a tremendous snowy owl. "Who?" he said as Letitia started to hop away in fright.

"Letitia Rabbit," said Letitia, ready to jump if he made a move toward her.

"Wait here, please," said the owl, and closed the door.

Letitia waited. High above her on the roof she heard the creaking of a weather vane. The door was opened again, this time by a tall and beautiful fair-haired lady in a shimmering green and gold dress. She looked worried. When she saw the ball of string her eyes opened wide. "You've brought back the song string!" she said. "Come in."

"The what string?" said Letitia as she hopped inside.

"The song string," said the lady. "You can't imagine all the trouble I've been having since that other rabbit ran off with it."

Letitia thought about that for a few moments while she stood looking up at the tall beautiful lady. "What's your name?" she asked.

"Miss Green," said the lady.

"Are you the real Miss Green?" asked Letitia. She told her about the Birch Hollow String Festival and how she was going to be Miss Green this year.

"Yes, I'm the real Miss Green," said Miss Green. She stopped looking worried long enough to laugh. "Mr. Largehop's great-great-great-grandfather wasn't very nice to hop off with my string and lock it up in a box," she said. "But you've brought it back now, and everything will be all right."

"Is it magic string?" said Letitia. "It *must* be magic, the way it led me here."

"I guess that was the first chance it had to get loose and come home," said Miss Green. "It isn't so very magic — it's for finding songs. Come on, I'll show you."

Letitia looked through the window at the full moon rising. "It's late," she said. "My mother and father are going to be worried about me."

Miss Green scribbled a note, opened the door, and whistled. A snowy owl appeared, took the note and flew away into the night. "I've told them you're visiting me and not to worry," said Miss Green.

They went outside, through the garden where the yew bears and wolves and owls glittered with frost in the moonlight and looked taller than they had at twilight. The fir trees moaned in the north wind, and and owl hooted nearby.

"Maybe I should wait for you in the house," said Letitia. "Maybe you need to be alone to look for a song."

"Oh, no," said Miss Green. "Please come along. I might need your help."

Letitia held tightly to a corner of Miss Green's cloak and stayed close to her as they went over frosty fields and patches of snow that squeaked under their feet. They came to the top of a little hill where the wind sighed in a clump of pines. Letitia did not feel very comfortable about being out in the open on a moonlit night.

"Nobody'll bother you while you're with me," said Miss Green. "Let's see if there's anything around here." She held one end of the string, said, "String, string, roll along, find a song," and threw the ball of string. It rolled a little way along the ground and stopped.

"That doesn't look like a song place," said Miss Green. She went to where the string had stopped, knelt, and listened with her ear close to the ground. "Nothing's happening," she said. "It isn't working for me anymore."

"What's supposed to happen?" said Letitia.

"Well, it always used to roll somewhere where there was a song," said Miss Green. "It used to find something with a song in it that I could hear if I listened very carefully. But there's no song here. *You* listen."

Letitia listened. "I can hear something," she said. "Some kind of a little song, very soft, under the snow. It's a tiny little sleeping-grass song."

"Sing it," said Miss Green.

Letitia sang:

When shall I be seen?
When shall I be green?
When will all the snow
Go?

"You could hear it and I couldn't," said Miss Green. "I'm just so tired from song-hunting year after year without the string that I'm all worn out. Now even when the string finds me a song I can't hear it. That's what your great-great-great-grandfather's done. It's all his fault." She began to cry.

"It wasn't *my* great-great-great-grandfather," said Letitia. "It was Mr. First Selectrabbit Largehop's. Anyhow, what's so bad about not being able to hear a song?"

"If I don't find a song I'll be late with spring," said Miss Green. She wiped her eyes and blew her nose.

"Did you say 'string'?" asked Letitia.

"No, I said 'spring,'" said Miss Green. "The season after winter."

"That's right," said Letitia. "String."

"Well, you can call it whatever you want," said Miss Green. "If I don't find a song that'll put Mr. Brumus to sleep it's going to be late."

"Who's Mr. Brumus?" asked Letitia.

"Come back to the house and you can meet him," said Miss Green.

When they got back to the house they went up to the top floor, to a very cold room with frost flowers on all the windows. There were weather maps on all the walls, and in the middle of the room was a blackboard with tomorrow's weather chalked up on it. Standing by the blackboard was Mr. Brumus. He was wearing a polar-bearskin coat, his long nose was red with the cold, and he was blowing out his breath in frosty clouds. He had cold-blue eyes behind rimless glasses, a sharp face, and long white hair. As he looked at the blackboard he turned a black iron wheel at the end of a black iron shaft that went up through the ceiling. When he turned the wheel the weather vane on the roof creaked.

"That's not an ordinary weather vane," said Miss Green to Letitia. "This one tells the wind which way to blow when Mr. Brumus turns the wheel. There'll be snow tomorrow. Ahem!" she said. "Mr. Brumus."

"What?" said Mr. Brumus without looking away from the black-board. "I'm busy."

"I'd like you to meet Letitia Rabbit," said Miss Green.

"How do you do," said Letitia.

"Cloudy and colder," said Mr. Brumus.

"Sing him your song," said Miss Green to Letitia.

Letitia sang the little sleeping-grass song.

"Heavy snow, followed by freezing rain," said Mr. Brumus, and chalked up more weather on the blackboard.

"Now you see what I have to go through," said Miss Green to Letitia. "Sometimes I sing him fifty or sixty different songs before I find the one that'll put him to sleep."

"Why do you have to put him to sleep?" said Letitia.

"Because he won't stop winter and I can't start spring until I do, that's why," said Miss Green. "As long as he's awake I'm stuck in the studio drawing snowflakes and frost flowers."

"You have to *draw* them?" said Letitia.

"Come up to the studio and I'll show you," said Miss Green.

In the studio were paints and brushes and a big worktable piled high with watercolor drawings of snowflakes. There were many more snowflake designs pinned to the walls. "I have to get through all this before I can start spring," said Miss Green. "Sometimes I think I'll never catch up, and I'm so tired of doing snowflakes!"

"Do you have to draw every single one that's going to fall?" asked Letitia.

"It's not quite that bad," said Miss Green. "I only have to do the first ones. The squirrels and the mice on the next floor down stamp out the patterns and the owls fly them up to get the clouds started. I draw the frost flowers too, and the squirrels go around and copy those on windows with their tails. But I'm so tired of winter!"

"What about string?" asked Letitia. "Spring, I mean."

"Spring is fun," said Miss Green. "Then it's *my* turn at the weather vane, and I set it for soft rains and warm breezes. I do the leaf and flower designs to show the trees and flowers how to look every year, I wake up the trees so the sap will run again, and I wake up the animals who sleep through the winter. I do all kinds of things I like to do, but I can't do any of them until Mr. Brumus goes to sleep, and sometimes he's just so stubborn I don't know what to do. Whatever song I sing, he just shakes his head and says more winter weather. Then he goes back to his blackboard and I have to do more snow-flakes. I'm so afraid I'll be late with spring this year."

"What are you going to do?" said Letitia.

"I was hoping you'd help me," said Miss Green.

"Me?" said Letitia.

"Well, I can't hear the songs the string finds anymore," said Miss Green. "And you can. Besides, it was a rabbit that helped get us into all this trouble, so I think a rabbit ought to help get us out."

"But I have to get home," said Letitia.

"Do you want to go home and tell them we're going to have winter all year because you wouldn't look for a song?" said Miss Green.

"We *can't* have winter all year," said Letitia. "String *always* comes."

"All right," said Miss Green. "Go on home. You'll see."

"You really think it won't come without a song?" said Letitia.

"It's never come without a song so far," said Miss Green. "I told you, first I sing Mr. Brumus to sleep and then I start in on spring. As long as he's awake you can expect winter weather."

"All right," said Letitia. "I'll stay until I find a song. Do you think it'll take long?"

"It *can't*," said Miss Green. "It's got to be soon, or the whole rest of the year will come out wrong. And it isn't as if you have to make up the song — you just have to find it. I'm sure that if you can do it this one time, I can do it by myself again next year — it's just that I'm so far behind and so anxious by now that the harder I try the less good it does."

"Well," said Letitia, "I *am* this year's Miss Green in Birch Hollow, and if you can't find a string song I guess I'll have to."

The next day she went out by herself, wearing a badge that Miss Green had pinned to her coat to show that she was doing spring work and was not to be bothered by foxes, weasels, owls, and other hunters. The snow that Mr. Brumus had chalked up yesterday had stopped falling, and now it was raining. Letitia hopped through the cold and the wet to the top of the hill where she had heard the little sleeping-

grass song. There she said the words and threw the ball of string.

The string took her to the little stream at the bottom of the hill. Letitia scraped away the wet snow and looked through the ice at the stones and twigs and brown leaves on the bottom of the stream. She listened to the water singing under the ice, and she hopped back to sing the song to Mr. Brumus.

Mr. Brumus was at his blackboard again.

"Ahem!" said Letitia. "Mr. Brumus?"

"What?" said Mr. Brumus without turning around. "I'm busy with sleet and hail."

"Song," said Letitia.

"Really," said Mr. Brumus. "I'm not a bit tired, and there's lots of winter work still to do. Miss Green always wants me to stop before

I'm ready. Everybody always waits for spring to come as if it were the only season that mattered, but there has to be winter too, you know. No one seems to care about my work or whether I get it done properly. I must say it hardly seems fair."

"Miss Green says that she has to help with the winter work, but you have to listen to songs when it gets to be this time of year," said Letitia. "She says that's how you always do it."

"Oh, all right," said Mr. Brumus, and he sat down in a chair. "Sing your song," he said.

Letitia sang:

Hear the stream in winter's keeping
Sing a quiet tune
Dreaming in its winter sleeping,
Spring is coming soon.
Leaf and stone are summer keeping
In the stream through winter sleeping,
Spring is coming soon.

Mr. Brumus closed his eyes and hummed along with the song. When Letitia had finished he opened his eyes and said, "Well, I suppose a little east wind wouldn't do any harm. And maybe some fog."

"He said east wind and fog," Letitia told Miss Green.

"That's *good!*" said Miss Green. "He's beginning to loosen up a little. You're gaining on him, Letitia. Look." She opened a cabinet and took out leaf and flower designs. "I've got the first ones all ready," she said.

"They're so gay and pretty," said Letitia.

"It'll soon be time for them," said Miss Green. "Not many days left."

"Don't tell me how many," said Letitia. "It'll just make me nervous."

Letitia went out in the fog the next day, determined to get warmer weather out of Mr. Brumus. The string took her to the pines on the hill. She listened to the song the wind was singing there and brought it back to Mr. Brumus:

Who
Is singing through
The boughs, singing still
On the hill,
Singing there
In the air,
Singing by?
It is I,
The spring wind waiting.

"It'll have to keep waiting," said Mr. Brumus. "I haven't quite finished with the north wind yet. Snow flurries tomorrow."

"He's so *stubborn*," said Miss Green when Letitia told her. "Several robins have arrived already, and they've been complaining to me."

"Well, it's only flurries, not a big snow," said Letitia. "But I'm beginning to wonder what it takes to put him to sleep."

"Patience and hard work," said Miss Green, and went back to drawing snowflakes.

Letitia took the ball of string and went out again. She went out the next day in the snow flurries and the day after that in high winds and cold rain. She went out in every kind of weather, and every day she brought back new songs that she sang to Mr. Brumus. But Mr. Brumus went on saying that he wasn't tired.

"Yes, you are, too," said Letitia one day when she was at the end of her patience. "I can see that you're tired, even if you can't. You have to work harder and harder to make cold weather. Your last snow flurries only lasted half an hour before the sun came out." She sang a teasing tune:

Mr. Brumus is tired,
Mr. Brumus is tired.

"*That* certainly won't get you anywhere," said Mr. Brumus, and the next day was bleak and bitter cold, with the wind whistling out of the north.

"Don't give up," chirped the forlorn early robins when they saw Letitia hop slowly by. But Letitia was feeling very low. She hopped into the woods, said the words, and threw the ball of string. Only

after she saw it go bounding away did she notice that she had not held on to the end of it. "Not that it makes much difference," she said, and began to cry.

When she had finished crying Letitia went to look for the string. While she was looking for it she smelled a fox. "It's a good thing I'm wearing my badge," she said to herself. Then she noticed that she wasn't wearing it. The badge had come unpinned and she had lost it.

"I'll have to run for it," said Letitia. She hopped away, while behind her and getting closer she heard the fox. He was singing, *"It's a hop, hop, hop, hop, rabbitty morning today."*

"He's got a song," said Letitia, "but he hasn't got me yet." She found a fallen tree that was hollow, hopped into it, and wriggled along until she was in a space too narrow for the fox to follow her into.

Letitia cried a little more then, sitting inside the hollow tree and listening for the fox. His footsteps came closer, and then she saw his face at the opening. He tried to squeeze in, could not, and settled down to wait outside, pacing up and down and singing a little song under his breath. Letitia could not hear all the words, but the chorus was *"Rabbit stew, rabbit stew."*

It was then that Letitia noticed some kind of a sound inside her

hollow tree. There was a smell inside it too. The smell was of honey and the sound was the buzzing of bees.

The bees were at the other end of the hollow tree, and they were in their winter cluster, singing and dancing to keep warm. The ones on the outside of the cluster were stamping their feet and beating their wings and singing the loudest while they waited for their turn to move to the inside where it was warmer. They were all singing at the top of their voices :

Bee my honey, honey my bee,
Sweet and cozy you and me.
Spring is coming,
Things are humming,
Bee my honey, honey my bee.
Buzz buzz buzz, buzz buzz buzz.

Letitia stopped crying. "Mr. Fox," she called.
"Here," said the fox.
"I'm Letitia Rabbit," said Letitia.
"If you don't mind," said the fox, "I prefer not to meet my lunches in a social way. You understand how it is."

"I'm the Letitia Rabbit who's helping Miss Green," said Letitia, "and if you don't let me out of here so I can take this song to Mr. Brumus you'll be holding up springtime."

"You're *that* rabbit!" said the fox. "I beg your pardon. You can come out. I'll go away. Word of honor."

"Thank you," said Letitia. She waited until the fox had gone, came slowly out of the hollow tree, looked and listened and sniffed all around to make sure that he had kept his word, then hopped back to the house. She made a cup of tea for Mr. Brumus and took it up to him.

"Ahem," she said.

"All right," said Mr. Brumus. He put down his chalk, left the blackboard, and sat down to listen.

"This is a song to you," said Letitia. "But instead of calling you Mr. Brumus in it I just call you B. Is that all right?"

"I don't mind," said Mr. Brumus.

Letitia had added some words of her own, and she sang:

Bee my honey, honey my bee,
Stop and have a cup of tea.

Mr. Brumus sipped his tea. "Nobody ever called me honey before," he said.

Letitia continued:

Now you've done your wintry best,
Put your feet up, take a rest.

Mr. Brumus put his feet up on a table. "I *have* been working hard," he said. "No question about it."

Letitia went on:

Bee my honey, honey my bee,
Sweet and cozy you and me
Spring is coming,
Things are humming.

Mr. Brumus closed his eyes. "Fair and warmer," he said drowsily. "Wind from the south. Tell Miss Green it's time to change the weather vane."

Letitia finished the song:

> *Be my honey, honey my bee.*
> *Buzz buzz buzz, buzz buzz buzz.*

Mr. Brumus was asleep in his chair. "I knew I had a winner with those bees," said Letitia, and went into the studio. "String is here," she said.

Miss Green smiled a big smile and sighed a big sigh of relief. Then she called all the downstairs squirrels, who very gently and carefully put Mr. Brumus to bed.

"So the string finally found the right song," she said.

"Oh, dear," said Letitia. "I forgot all about the string. I better go look for it."

"I think it'll probably look for you," said Miss Green.

"That's right," said Letitia. "It *is* a magic string, really. Even though it didn't find the song."

"Nothing's magic *all* the time," said Miss Green. "And even if the string didn't find a song it found me a song finder. It found me you." She hugged and kissed Letitia and walked her back to Birch Hollow.

Miss Green said good-bye at the bottom of the hill behind Letitia's house. "When you want to visit me the string will show you the way again," she said.

When Letitia went up the hill she found the ball of string looking as new as ever, with the end of it wrapped around the tree where she had once tied it.

"Letitia," called Mrs. Rabbit from the house, "you'll have to stop practicing with that string long enough to try on the dress so we can see how it fits."

"Here I come," said Letitia. While she was putting on the dress and had it over her head she heard her mother say, "Good heavens!"

"What's the matter?" said Letitia.

"There was a great big white owl at the window just now," said Mrs. Rabbit, "and he's left a note." She opened the window. "Lovely day," she said. "It's much warmer than it was."

"What does the note say?" said Letitia.

"Happy Stringtime!" read Mrs. Rabbit.

"Happy Stringtime to you too," said Letitia.

About the Author

Since the publication of *Bedtime for Frances* in 1960 Russell Hoban's books have gradually come to occupy a place of their own in children's literature.

A Bargain for Frances, *Bread and Jam for Frances*, and other stories about the lovable song-spinning badger, and *Emmet Otter's Jug Band Christmas* have been praised for their "uncloying gentleness" and "forthrightness" as well as for the fresh, multileveled humor that characterizes all of Mr. Hoban's stories.

Clifton Fadiman, in his thoughtful article on "Children's Literature" in the latest edition of the *Encyclopaedia Britannica*, described *The Mouse and His Child* as ". . . flawlessly written . . . [with] an unforgettable assortment of terribly real, humanized animals," and compared Mr. Hoban's story to long-established classics such as *Alice in Wonderland* and *The Borrowers*.

Russell Hoban lives in England. He has recently completed his first novel since *The Mouse and His Child*.

About the Artist

Mary Chalmers says, "Aside from books and art, the great love of my life has been animals."

She has written and illustrated several delightful books for children, including *A Christmas Story*. Miss Chalmers has illustrated, among others, *When Will It Snow?*, *Throw a Kiss, Harry*, and *The Snuggle Bunny*.

Her love of animals, so clearly reflected by her charming drawings, has led Mary Chalmers to do volunteer work at the local animal shelter, near her home in Haddon Heights, New Jersey, for the past several years.

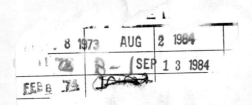
Me